To my mother: the first person to read this "angry rant" back in 2020. Thank you for not asking me to quiet down, but instead telling me that this was the "slap in the face" the world needed to finally wake up and see African women.

A Letter to Feminists

Copyright © 2021 by Nate Haliv.

For inquiries: natehaliv@gmail.com

All rights reserved. No part of this book may be reproduced, transmitted, or stored in an information retrieval system in any form or by any means, graphic, electronic, or mechanical, including photocopying, taping, and recording, without prior written permission from the author.

This book is a work of combined genres. The sections are works of social commentary and non-fiction. They reflect the personal opinions, research, and experiences of the author. References to historical figures, public figures, organizations (such as Amnesty International, UNICEF, IOM), and news outlets are used for educational and critical purposes.

The narrative sections featuring the character Aisha Okorie are works of fiction inspired by actual events. While the protagonist and specific incidents are products of the author's imagination or used fictitiously, the context regarding human trafficking routes, the conditions in Libya, and the "Madam" systems in Europe are based on documented reports and composite accounts of real survivors. Any resemblance to actual persons, living or dead, or actual events is purely coincidental, except where explicitly stated as historical fact.

All product names, logos, and brands (e.g., The Guardian, BBC, Davido, Wizkid) are property of their respective owners. All company, product, and service names used in this book are for identification purposes only.

NATE HALIV: A LETTER TO FEMINISTS

This is not a scholarly article. It is a genre-blending "angry rant," written to be understood not just by those in academia, but also by young Black African girls who have long felt invisible in feminist discourse. Many of these girls have been denied a formal education, and they are the reason I am writing this—though some might call it a manifesto.

I have intentionally adopted a conversational tone to keep this message accessible to them. This choice is by design, not due to any lack of scholarly ability; I refuse to alienate the very women I am writing to protect by hiding behind dense academic jargon.

Many feminists, activists, and organizations proclaim that human rights have no borders. We see countless demonstrations against injustices in the U.S. and Europe, protests like Black Lives Matter for George Floyd's murder in 2020, which spread to over 60 countries (according to The Guardian), including my country, Nigeria, which seemed quite ironic to me because of the high level of tribalism in the country, but that's a conversation for another day. German football players have actively protested human rights abuses and demonstrated support for LGBTQ+ rights.

For instance, the team advocated for rainbow armbands during the UEFA Euro 2020 tournament in direct response to Hungary's anti-LGBT legislation. Later, players covered their mouths in team photos at the Qatar World Cup to protest the ban on OneLove armbands.

Despite this visible activism, the mistreatment of African or Muslim women in certain Middle Eastern countries rarely ignites a similar level of global outcry.

- Saudi Arabia only lifted its driving ban for women in 2018 (BBC, June 2018).
- In another Middle Eastern country, women are still prohibited from traveling to other cities without a male chaperone. Imagine being a

woman and not legally allowed to travel from New York City to Dallas for a business meeting without having a male chaperone. Sounds awkward, right?

Where is the uproar when these very real restrictions on women's basic freedoms continue? If feminism is a collective movement, why does this fervor vanish at the borders of Africa or the Middle East? Why is the world quiet about the eurocentrism of feminism?

According to a 2016 Amnesty International report, roughly 40,000 children, some as young as 7 years old, were believed to be working in artisanal mines in the Democratic Republic of Congo to extract cobalt or coltan used in electronics. Congo produces 70% of the cobalt in the world.

These children, many of them girls, work amid constant dangers: collapsing mine shafts, toxic dust, and exposure to chemicals that can lead to long-term illnesses, including cancer. They work in mines for at least 8 hours a day while being exposed to harmful toxins only to earn less than $1. If that isn't the definition of "cruelty," then I don't know what is.

Imagine the global outrage if seven-year-old German or American girls were being exploited in the same way by African companies and forced to work in mines. News outlets and activists would be on high alert.

However, because these are Congolese girls, their stories barely make headlines. Many people don't even know that there is a country named "Congo." Yet, without Congo, they probably wouldn't be using a cell phone.

Even certain foreign NGOs in the DRC remain silent, fearing repercussions from the government or the loss of lucrative partnerships with powerful stakeholders in the coltan industry. But true advocacy demands that we name and condemn such exploitation, rather than remain "neutral."

We see widespread calls to boycott fashion brands for using real animal fur, yet the response to child labor in African mines is comparatively muted.

Why not threaten to boycott phone manufacturers who knowingly benefit from resources mined through child labor? If we truly believe in feminism without borders, then these young voices, risking their lives for the minerals powering our devices, must be heard, defended, and prioritized.

A 2023 study noted **that artisanal miners have five times higher concentrations of toxic metals (uranium and mercury) in their urine** compared to non-miners.

Imagine your 8-year-old daughter or granddaughter working in a mine where she could get exposed to various infections and illnesses. Sad, right? Yet mainstream feminist platforms rarely champion these girls.

Let's talk about Female Genital Mutilation (FGM), a missing subject during my Bachelor's and Master's degrees. I heard the name Betty Friedan in almost all my courses. She was the middle-class white woman with a "problem with no name," and I wrote so many assignments on her that I probably mentioned her in my sleep.

Yet there was absolutely nothing in the syllabus about the Black girls in Africa whose vaginas were being cut shortly after birth.

According to UNICEF, at least 200 million girls and women globally have undergone FGM, with the majority living in Africa and parts of the Middle East. Many are cut as infants or at a very young age, leading to lifelong trauma, infections, and complications in childbirth. **In Somalia, the prevalence of FGM among women aged 15–49 is 99%**. In Guinea, it is 95%. In Djibouti, it is 90%.

Yet this crisis seldom dominates global feminist headlines or academic syllabi. Instead, popular discourse fixates on media trends like celebrity feminist branding, hashtag activism, and surface-level cultural representation—important in their own way, but they often overshadow a life-or-death epidemic for millions of women.

According to 2022 United Nations data, Africa is home to over 1.4 billion people. Women make up roughly half of this population, amounting to at least 700 million individuals. In sub-Saharan Africa specifically, many of these women are subject to patriarchal traditions, extreme poverty, and limited access to education.

- **Education Gaps:** UNESCO estimates that around 9 million girls in sub-Saharan Africa between the ages of 6 and 11 will never attend school.
- **Forced Early Marriage:** According to UNICEF, around 40% of girls in sub-Saharan Africa are married before their 18th birthday.

We must confront the stark gap between mainstream feminist discourse and the lived realities of women who lack basic human rights—women who face ritual violence, forced marriage, trafficking, or denial of education solely because they are female.

There is no denying the severity of poverty across Africa. According to World Bank estimates, over 570 million Africans live in extreme poverty, defined as surviving on less than $1.90 per day, and many cannot afford even $3 a day for basic needs. This figure could be higher if measured against European standards of poverty, but it nonetheless reflects a staggering crisis.

Compounding these hardships is a **deeply ingrained belief in "Juju,"** where some individuals cling to the notion that rituals or occult practices can grant sudden wealth.

In Nigeria alone, millions reportedly adhere to this idea, while local tabloids and social media pages (like Instablog9ja) frequently report crimes tied to ritual killings, fraud, and violent acts against women and children. These ritualistic killing acts often target four vulnerable groups—albinos, hunchbacks, pregnant women, and young children (sometimes as young as three years old).

The horror is unimaginable: an innocent child, just beginning life, sacrificed by someone seeking financial gain without legitimate work.

I genuinely wonder why this tragic reality rarely surfaces in mainstream feminist discourse. Mainstream feminism often dissects every nuance of the white, Western female experience yet minimizes or ignores the existential crises facing Black women in Africa. **It creates a dynamic that essentially says: "My problems are our problems. But your problems? Those are just yours."**

Something else that has been bothering me since I picked up my first text on feminism, Judith Butler's "Gender Trouble," is the absence of Black African women from university curriculums.

Why do equally remarkable African women who fought against both colonialism and patriarchy receive so little attention in mainstream feminist scholarship?

When African women are included in the curriculum, they are often those whose works align with Eurocentric frameworks rather than reflecting the lived realities of hundreds of millions of women across the continent.

These authors are embraced because they do not subvert the white hierarchy; they are tolerated precisely because they do not challenge dominant Western norms.

Take **Funmilayo Ransome-Kuti** (1900–1978), often referred to as the "Mother of African Women's Rights." She organized unions, campaigned for women's suffrage in colonial Nigeria, and later challenged military dictatorships.

Archival records from the Funmilayo Ransome-Kuti Papers confirm that she not only vehemently opposed unjust taxes targeting women but also participated in the constitutional conferences that shaped Nigeria's independence.

Tragically, she died from injuries inflicted by the same nation she fought for, after being thrown from a window during a Nigerian military raid intended to silence her family's advocacy.

Yet, in many feminist syllabi, her name is missing. This is the woman who stood against British colonial tyranny, challenged the Alake of Abeokuta's exploitative tax regime, forcing the king to abdicate his throne and go into temporary exile during an era of suffocating patriarchy in Nigeria. This same woman fought for female suffrage in Nigeria, securing voting rights for women, which rippled across Africa. She organized literacy classes for girls whose fathers saw them only as future wives, all while raising her son, the pioneer of Afrobeats, Fela Kuti.

If a résumé like that isn't enough, I have to ask: What else should Funmilayo Ransome-Kuti have done to be included in the feminist discourse? Personally put a bullet in Hitler's head?

Similarly absent from typical feminist studies is **Gisèle Rabesahala** of Madagascar, who became a politician at age 17 and championed political prisoners' rights. She formed the first Malagasy political party led by a woman, never married, and rejected the societal expectation to have children, an especially bold stance in a cultural context where motherhood often defines a woman's worth. Needless to say, Rabesahala is absent from the mainstream feminist discourse.

Another glaring omission is **Yaa Asantewaa** (circa 1840–1921) of the Ashanti Kingdom in modern-day Ghana. The British governor of the Gold Coast demanded to sit on or control the Golden Stool, which was the most sacred symbol of Ashanti authority, unity, and the soul of the nation. The Ashanti saw this demand as a grave insult and a direct threat to their sovereignty and identity. Queen Mother Yaa Asantewaa led the Ashanti people and fought fiercely to protect their sacred stool and resist colonial interference.

Although the British eventually suppressed the uprising and extended colonial rule over Ashanti territory, they never captured the Golden Stool, which remained hidden and protected by the Ashanti people.

Of course, mainstream feminist courses would rather focus on the white woman "trapped" in a house with a microwave and facing a nameless problem than canonize a Black woman who led a war against the tyranny of the colonial British empire.

Imagine if a European woman had single-handedly led a resistance that defeated Adolf Hitler; she would likely be romanticized and memorialized in every major history textbook.

This pattern of erasure is not limited to historical figures. Contemporary icons such as **Wangari Maathai**, the first African woman to receive the Nobel Peace Prize (2004), or **Ngozi Okonjo-Iweala**, the first woman and first African to lead the World Trade Organization (WTO) (2021), rarely appear with the same frequency as their Western counterparts in many feminist studies syllabi.

Similarly, **Miriam Makeba** ("Mama Africa") and **Folorunso Alakija** (one of Africa's most successful businesswomen) are household names in parts of Africa, yet they remain peripheral in typical Western academic discourse.

Compare this to how Betty Friedan's 1963 publication, The Feminine Mystique (W. W. Norton & Company), is treated. Her work on the "nameless problem" of domestic confinement for middle-class white American women is routinely taught as foundational.

Meanwhile, African women who simultaneously confronted colonialism, repressive military regimes, racism, classism, and patriarchal oppression, often at the cost of their freedom or lives, are overlooked.

It is striking that figures who could not initially name their "problem" gain global recognition, whereas African women, like Funmilayo Ransome-Kuti or Yaa Asantewaa, who waged multifaceted battles (against colonial powers, military regimes, and entrenched misogyny) remain obscure.

God knows the thousands of girls forced to work at coltan mines in Congo would rather be "trapped in a home" with a microwave, television, and a fridge and deal with "a problem that has no name" than continue surviving the hell of their current reality.

This selective visibility is precisely what spurred me to write **"Seeing the World Through a Black Woman's Eyes," "Lucy Far: The Untold Story of Child Trafficking,"** and **"The Girl Who Ran Without Legs."** I am angry at the ways African women's struggles are minimized and overlooked, and I am exhausted by the silence surrounding their lived realities. I am tired of curriculums that only include books by African women who do not challenge dominant Western narratives—books focused on "accents" and "hair politics," topics that 99% of women on the African continent cannot relate to.

According to data from the Nigeria Deposit Insurance Corporation (NDIC), approximately 99.4% of bank accounts in Nigeria hold less than five hundred thousand naira ($347) as of 2024. Note that at the time I revised this text, **Nigeria, a country filled with 230 million people, where 99.4% of its citizens don't have up as much as $347, is statistically the 4th largest economy in Africa.** There are 54 countries in Africa. If this is the reality in a "top tier" African economy, imagine the rest.

How exactly do women who do not even have $347 in their bank accounts worry about "accent problems" abroad? Yet, this is what the dominant Western feminist narrative offers its students as the "African experience"—a narrative that the vast majority of African women cannot recognize. Is the 8-year-old girl working in a coltan mine in the Congo worrying about "accents"? Or the women in the Igbo community in Nigeria branded as "Osu?"

Young girls are victims of the **Igbo "Osu" caste system** here in Nigeria. They, along with their future daughters for thousands of generations, are rendered outcasts, unable to marry freely within the community, condemned to be born into discrimination, and destined to die in it. Imagine you and your future generations being condemned to live as pariahs in your own community simply because your ancestors, perhaps 10 to 15 generations ago, were dedicated to deities or considered slaves.

Sex trafficking of African teenagers, particularly "light-skinned girls younger than 20" from West Africa to Italy, is glaringly absent in the feminist curriculum.

Yet the numbers are impossible to ignore. At the peak of the crisis (2016–2018), the International Organization for Migration (IOM) reported that **over 80% of Nigerian women arriving in Italy by sea were likely victims of trafficking for sexual exploitation.** I will elaborate on this in the next section.

Frankly, I want to grab a cup of matcha and listen to Davido's Timeless album right now, just to calm my brain before it explodes. Writing about the way women who look like your mother, sisters, and daughters are erased from the educational stratosphere takes a heavy toll.

I will round off this note with a simple question: Dear feminists, are African women part of the global feminist agenda or not? Pick a side.

Until African women's rights are as fiercely championed as those of Western women, I refuse to believe the claim that feminism is truly inclusive.

A LETTER TO FEMINISTS by NATE HALIV

Greener Pastures? More Like Darker Pastures: The Mirage of the Migrant Dream

Now that I have finished drinking my matcha and my brain is relatively calm, let me continue my "rants."

The caffeine has settled; Davido's "Away" is playing on my speakers, and the warmth of the tea has provided a momentary respite; yet the subject matter I must now address offers no such comfort.

This part of my letter is addressed to the thousands of African women who hope to escape difficult economic conditions by migrating to Europe. It is a letter written in ink, but it is inspired by stories written in blood.

Many are unaware of the danger of sex trafficking along the way, a topic I explore in the story of my protagonist in **Seeing the World Through a Black Woman's Eyes**, Aisha Okorie.

Aisha's experiences shed light on a harsh reality: the journey can be fatal, and upon arrival, women can find themselves indebted to traffickers, trapped in cycles of forced prostitution or other forms of exploitation.

The realities of life in many African countries, including Nigeria, can be daunting, especially for young people seeking opportunities to thrive.

From dysfunctional social systems to grueling economic conditions, these challenges often push individuals to consider leaving their home countries in search of better lives.

Yet for many who embark on such journeys, the promise of prosperity in Europe can quickly turn into a tragic tale of human trafficking, forced prostitution, and modern slavery.

Sex trafficking is a massive global enterprise. According to the International Labour Organization (ILO), around 4.8 million people are trapped in forced sexual exploitation worldwide.

Nigeria's Edo State, often called the sex trafficking hub of West Africa, is notorious for networks that funnel young women into European countries under false promises of decent-paying work.

Disturbing reports from CNN and Amnesty International indicate the existence of **slave markets in Libya, where migrants can be bought and sold for as little as $400**. Women are vulnerable to forced labor or sex slavery.

Some never reach Europe at all, vanishing into these grim realities after being deceived by traffickers. These women, referred to as "madams," who are often former trafficking victims themselves, evolve into powerful brokers of exploitation. They coordinate with smugglers, arrange perilous crossings, and command a sophisticated web of intimidation. Many of these madams operate in Italy, Spain, and other parts of Europe, counting on fear and superstition to keep their victims silent. In some heartbreaking cases, parents knowingly send their daughters abroad, aware they will work in prostitution.

Driven by grinding poverty, these families see no alternative but to survive, hoping that once the daughter repays her debt, she can send money home.

Nigeria is Africa's most populous country, with over 230 million citizens, and is blessed with abundant natural resources. However, systemic corruption, nepotism, and weak social services drive countless Nigerians into a state of perpetual frustration. Let's examine some of the key factors fueling the desperation to leave:

- **Academic and Professional Hurdles:** Gaining entrance into Nigerian universities can be prohibitively difficult if you lack influential connections. It often doesn't matter how brilliant or talented you are; if you do not have the right social network (like if your father is not a close friend of any professor at the university you wish to study), you may be denied admission to competitive fields such as medicine, law, and nursing. Once you do secure a job, low wages and exploitative conditions are common. As of 2018, the minimum wage was roughly 30,000 naira ($20 per month), later increased to 70,000 naira ($48 based on the current exchange rate), yet many employers still pay below this threshold. Overtime pay is practically non-existent; complain too much, and you might be fired. In a country with millions of unemployed citizens, your boss can easily replace you.

- **Healthcare Gaps:** Most Nigerians are not covered by any health insurance plan, and many don't even know what health insurance is. This means if you fall ill or end up in an accident, you may be denied treatment until your bills are paid in full. Countless lives are lost to treatable conditions simply because families cannot gather funds quickly enough. Even a minor surgical procedure can bankrupt an entire household.

- **Energy and Infrastructure Deficits:** Some neighborhoods endure months, if not years, without reliable power. The alternative is to buy expensive fuel to run generators, compounding the financial strain. In many European countries, one can buy goods in installments. In Nigeria, nearly everything must be paid for outright in cash, making it tough to access essential items, from electronics to business supplies.

- **Gender Discrimination:** As a woman, you might be expected to exchange sexual favors just to secure a job or maintain a position. Reporting such abuse can be futile, given rampant corruption and victim-blaming. By age 20, families often begin pressuring women to marry rather than continue their education. This stifles personal growth and makes it even harder to find economic stability on one's own terms.

Faced with these daunting realities, it's no surprise many Nigerians dream of emigrating to Europe or North America, imagining a place where minimum wage laws are upheld, healthcare is accessible, and educational opportunities abound.

According to the World Bank, remittances from the Nigerian diaspora were around $17.2 billion in 2020.

This shows how many Nigerians successfully leave and send money back home. Yet behind the success stories, there are also countless tragedies.

When I sat down to write **Lucy Far: The Untold Story of Child Trafficking** and **Seeing the World Through a Black Woman's Eyes**, my intention was to capture the visceral, often silent reality of the African female experience. I wanted to move beyond the statistics and headlines to touch the human pulse of suffering and resilience.

In **Seeing the World Through a Black Woman's Eyes**, my protagonist, Aisha Okorie, makes a decision that thousands of young Nigerian women make every year. She decides to leave.

Driven by the crushing weight of economic stagnation and the seductive promise of a European paradise, she places her life in the hands of a "sponsor."

Aisha's story is fiction, but the horror she endures is not. Her journey is a composite of the terrified whispers, police reports, and testimonies of thousands of women who have walked the road from Edo State to the shores of Italy.

I wrote Aisha's narrative as a cautionary tale because the gap between the dream of migration and the reality of human trafficking is a graveyard filled with the unrecovered bodies of the hopeful.

The Economic Push and the "Madam" Trap

To understand why a character like Aisha, or a real woman from Benin City, would risk death to leave home, one must first look at the economic landscape.

Nigeria is the giant of Africa, yet **according to the National Bureau of Statistics (NBS), over 133 million Nigerians are classified as multidimensionally poor**. The unemployment rate has historically hovered at alarming levels, with youth unemployment specifically reaching over 42% in recent years.

In my book, Aisha encounters a character named Madam Osasumwen. To Aisha, this woman appears as a savior, a benevolent matriarch offering a ticket to lawful employment and dignity in Europe. This is the first and perhaps most fatal deception.

In the real world, these "sponsors" are the linchpins of transnational criminal syndicates. The United Nations Office on Drugs and Crime (UNODC) has extensively documented this modus operandi. They do not present themselves as traffickers. They present themselves as helpers.

The tragedy is that the victims are often "recruited" by people they know. It might be a neighbor, a distant aunt, or a friend of the family who returns from Europe wearing designer clothes, spinning tales of easy money.

They target young women from regions like Edo State, which the International Organization for Migration (IOM) identified as a primary origin point for Nigerian women trafficked to Italy.

Between 2014 and 2016 alone, the number of Nigerian women arriving in Italy by sea surged by over 600%, with the IOM estimating that 80% of these arrivals were likely victims of trafficking for sexual exploitation.

The Invisible Graveyard of the Sahara

In the novel, Aisha's journey begins not on a boat, but in the back of a truck crossing the Sahara Desert. This is a part of the migration narrative that often goes unspoken because the cameras are rarely there to witness it. We see the footage of capsized boats in the Mediterranean, but we do not see the skeletons in the sand.

The journey usually involves passing through Agadez in Niger, a historical gateway to the Sahara. The conditions are subhuman. Migrants are packed into pickup trucks, hundreds at a time, with little water, racing across dunes to avoid patrols. If a passenger falls off the truck, the smugglers rarely stop. To stop is to risk arrest or delay.

Data from the IOM's "Missing Migrants Project" paints a grim picture. Since 2014, they have recorded over 5,900 deaths in the Sahara Desert. However, the IOM freely admits that this figure is a gross underestimation.

Unlike the sea, where bodies may eventually wash ashore, the desert swallows evidence. Experts and survivors suggest that for every person who drowns in the Mediterranean, at least two die in the desert from dehydration, exposure, or violence at the hands of smugglers.

Aisha witnesses this in my story. She watches fellow travelers collapse, never to rise again. It is a quiet, dusty death that barely registers as a statistic in the Western world.

The Libyan Bottleneck

If the desert is a graveyard, Libya is a prison. Upon surviving the Sahara, migrants enter a country fractured by civil war and ruled by militias. Reports from Amnesty International and CNN in 2017 shocked the world with footage of "slave markets" where African migrants were being auctioned off for as little as $400. This is the reality Aisha faces.

In Libya, the commodification of human life is total. Migrants are often held in detention centers, some of which are run by the state, others by militias.

The conditions are horrific. Overcrowding, starvation, and systematic rape are used as tools of extortion. Families back in Nigeria are contacted by phone and forced to listen to their daughters screaming while being tortured, a tactic designed to compel relatives to send more money.

When they are finally put on boats to cross the Mediterranean, the danger shifts but does not lessen. The boats are often flimsy, rubber dinghies unsuited for the high seas. The United Nations High Commissioner for Refugees (UNHCR) estimated that in 2021 alone, some 1,550 people died or went missing attempting to cross the Central Mediterranean.

My character, Aisha, loses her son during a violent encounter between smugglers and the Libyan Coast Guard. This plot point was difficult to write, but it reflects a common tragedy.

The European Union has funded the Libyan Coast Guard to intercept migrants, yet human rights groups have repeatedly documented that these interceptions often result in migrants being returned to the very detention centers where they face torture.

The Debt Bondage in Europe

There is a pervasive myth that reaching Italy means the suffering ends. In Seeing the World Through a Black Woman's Eyes, Aisha kisses the ground when she arrives in Italy, believing she is free. She is wrong. She has simply moved from the transport phase of trafficking to the exploitation phase.

Upon arrival, the benevolent mask of Madam Osasumwen slips. Aisha is informed that she owes a debt for her travel expenses. In real-world trafficking cases involving Nigerian networks, this debt is staggering, typically ranging from €30,000 to €50,000.

It is a sum that is mathematically impossible to pay off through legitimate low-wage work, even if the migrant had legal papers, which they almost never do.

This is where the coercion becomes total. The Madam informs the girl that there is no job as a hairdresser or a nanny. There is only "the street." To repay a debt of €30,000 while earning a fraction of that per transaction, a woman must service hundreds, sometimes thousands, of clients.

Aisha describes sleeping with up to ten men a day. This is not an exaggeration; it is the industrial scale of sexual exploitation required to service the debt. If she refuses, the violence is immediate. But often, physical violence is not even necessary because of a far more potent psychological weapon: Juju.

The Psychology of Control: Juju and Oaths

One of the most complex aspects of the Nigerian trafficking phenomenon is the use of traditional oaths, often referred to as "Juju." In the book, I explore how this spiritual mechanism binds Aisha to her trafficker more securely than any physical chain could.

Before leaving Nigeria, victims are often taken to a shrine by their recruiter. There, in the presence of a traditional priest, they perform a ritual.

They hand over personal items, including fingernails, hair, undergarments, and swear an oath of secrecy and obedience. They vow to repay their debt and never to report their Madam to the police. The belief is that breaking this oath will result in madness, death, or the mysterious illness of family members back home.

Western observers often dismiss this as mere superstition, but for the women involved, the threat is terrifyingly real. It acts as a psychological prison. This is a major reason why Italian and Spanish police struggle to prosecute Nigerian trafficking rings.

You can rescue a woman from the street, but you cannot easily rescue her from the fear that her disobedience will kill her mother in Benin City.

Furthermore, the threat is not purely spiritual. Trafficking networks are highly organized criminal enterprises, akin to the mafia. They have tentacles that reach back to the villages in Nigeria. If a victim in Turin or Palermo stops paying, thugs in Nigeria can be sent to pay a visit to her parents. The combination of spiritual terror and physical threat creates a wall of silence that is nearly impenetrable.

The Reality of the "Irregular Migrant"

Let us strip away the fiction for a moment and look at the administrative reality of Europe. If a young woman manages to escape her trafficker, what awaits her? She is an undocumented immigrant in a continent that is becoming increasingly hostile to migration.

Without valid documentation, she is an "irregular migrant." This status strips her of basic human rights. She cannot legally sign an employment contract. She cannot easily rent an apartment. In many cases, she cannot access non-emergency healthcare. She exists in a legal limbo.

The economic reality of Europe is harsh. The youth unemployment rate in countries like Italy and Spain is high even for citizens.

For an undocumented African woman who likely does not speak the language fluently, the options are nonexistent. This pushes many back into the arms of exploitative employers or back into sex work simply to survive. The European Union Agency for Fundamental Rights has noted that undocumented migrants are at extreme risk of severe labor exploitation because they cannot report abuse without risking deportation.

In the novel, Aisha lives with the constant, gnawing anxiety of deportation. This is a daily reality for thousands. A police siren is not a sound of safety; it is a sound of doom.

The psychological toll is immense. Studies on migrant populations frequently show elevated rates of post-traumatic stress disorder (PTSD), anxiety, and depression. They have survived the desert and the sea only to live in a state of permanent fear.

Okay, Let's Wrap Things Up

I wrote *Lucy Far: The Untold Story of Child Trafficking and Seeing the World Through a Black Woman's Eyes* not just to tell a story, but to sound an alarm. Thousands of girls like Kemisola Falade (Lucy Far) are taken from their families every year and their organs are forcefully taken from them. Their kidneys are sold on the black market. They are turned into "walking blood bags." They are even forced to work in prostitution rings to serve the needs of men who want to have sex with "young blood." Young blood here refers to girls under the age of ten. Some of these sexual predators are our professors in the university, our pastors in church, and our neighbors who help babysit our kids.

On the other hand, the character of Aisha Okorie serves as a vessel for the agony of a generation that is being sold a lie. The "greener pastures" of Europe are often fertilized with the blood of the innocent.

If you are a young woman in Nigeria reading this, or if you know someone who is making plans to travel with a "sponsor" who promises the world but demands secrecy, I beg you to look at the facts.

The International Labour Organization (ILO) estimates that there are 4.8 million people trapped in forced sexual exploitation worldwide. Do not become a number in that ledger. Investigate the legal channels. They are difficult, yes. The rejection rates for visas are high.

But the alternative is a gamble with your life where the house almost always wins. There are legitimate organizations, scholarships, verified work permits, and NGOs like the IOM that can provide truthful information.

If an offer sounds too good to be true, it is a trap. If someone tells you that you can travel without papers and they will "handle everything" for a fee you will pay later, you are being recruited into modern slavery. The debt they place on your head will be a shackle that may take years of abuse to break, if you survive at all.

We must stop romanticizing the exit. We have to confront the systems at home that make leaving feel like the only option, just as we must expose the criminal networks abroad that feast on our desperation.

The grass on the other side isn't greener. Often, it is a mirage, and by the time you realize you are standing on barren sand, it is too late to turn back.

Stay safe. Stay informed. Stay alive.

I do not have the scholarly weight of Michel Foucault nor the poetic grace of Shakespeare. I'm just a guy who wants his daughter to open a textbook and see women with her skin color staring back at her. I hope this message falls on the right ear.

Nate Haliv

OTHER BOOKS BY THE AUTHOR

- Lucy Far: The Untold Story of Child Trafficking
- Seeing the World Through a Black Woman's Eyes
- The Nigerian Prince

SOURCES & FURTHER READING

On mining in the Congo and child labor

Amnesty International. "This is What We Die For: Human rights abuses in the Democratic Republic of the Congo power the global trade in cobalt." Amnesty International, January 2016 — documents hazardous conditions in cobalt mines where thousands of children work under perilous conditions.

https://www.amnesty.org/en/documents/afr62/3183/2016/en/

On migration deaths (Sahara & Mediterranean)

International Organization for Migration (IOM). Missing Migrants Project – Mediterranean and global data — ongoing data on migrants who have died or gone missing on migration routes, including Mediterranean crossings and Saharan desert journeys.

https://missingmigrants.iom.int/

On the scale of migrant fatalities

Reuters (2024). "More than 63,000 people dead or missing while migrating over last decade, IOM says" — reporting on major trends in deaths and disappearances recorded by IOM's Missing Migrants Project since 2014.

https://www.reuters.com/world/more-than-63000-people-dead-or-missing-while-migrating-over-last-decade-iom-says-2024-03-26/

On child labor in cobalt mining (supplementary coverage)

Is my phone powered by child labour? — Amnesty International coverage explaining how child labor in DRC cobalt mining affects global supply chains and consumer electronics.

https://www.amnesty.org/en/latest/campaigns/2016/06/drc-cobalt-child-labour/

On broader migration mortality statistics

Migration data portal. Migrant deaths and disappearances — contextualizes IOM Missing Migrants Project data on deaths/disappearances worldwide.

https://www.migrationdataportal.org/themes/migrant-deaths-and-disappearances

Made in the USA
Coppell, TX
01 February 2026